A Surprise in the Mailbox

By Eleanor Fremont
Based on a Teleplay by Andy Yerkes
Illustrated by Tom Leigh

Simon Spotlight

Based on the TV series *Bear in the Big Blue House*™
created by Mitchell Kriegman. Produced by
The Jim Henson Company for Disney Channel.

 SIMON SPOTLIGHT
An imprint of Simon & Schuster Children's Publishing Division
1230 Avenue of the Americas
New York, New York 10020

Manufactured in the United States of America
First Edition   10 9 8 7 6 5 4
ISBN 0-689-82336-3

One sunny day, Bear and his friend Tutter went out to the mailbox in front of the Big Blue House.

"I wonder what came in the mail today," said Bear. "Maybe there's a postcard from a faraway place. Or maybe a magazine!"

"Look, Tutter!" Bear exclaimed. "Here's something for you."
"For me, Bear? A letter for me?" said Tutter. "Who's it from?"
Bear read the words in the corner of the envelope. "It looks like it's from your Grandma Flutter!"
"Grandma Flutter! My favorite grandma! Open it up, Bear! Open it up!" cried Tutter, jumping up and down.

Getting a letter is exciting, isn't it?

"What's it say, Bear? What's it say?" asked Tutter.

"It says that she's coming for a visit," read Bear.

"My grandma? Visiting me? Oh, boy! When?" said Tutter.

Bear read a little more. "Let me see," he said. "Oh, my. She's coming today!"

Tutter jumped up in surprise. "Today! But I'm not ready! Not ready at all! I haven't cleaned up! What will she think?"

"I'm sure everything will be fine," said Bear. "She just wants to see you. That's the important thing."

"But, Bear, you don't know her. She's very particular! She's clean, clean, clean!"

Tutter swept as fast as he could. He made so much noise that Pip and Pop came in to see what was the matter. And a moment later, in came Ojo, too.

"What'll I do? What'll I do?" Tutter worried out loud.

"I have an idea," said Bear. "Why don't we all work together? Then we can get this place cleaned up in no time!"

"Great!" said Tutter.

So they all cleaned up the house. They shined, they rubbed . . .

they dusted . . .

and scrubbed.

And when they were done, the house sparkled like a
new penny.

"Hey, Bear," said Pip, "is there anything else we can do—"
"To help get ready for Tutter's Grandma?" Pop finished.
"Hmm," said Bear. "Well, I guess you could weed the flower bed."
"We love weeds!" yelled Pip and Pop.
"I'll help too!" said Ojo.

While Pip and Pop and Ojo weeded,

Tutter tidied up his mouse hole.

"Have to make things clean, clean, clean!" he said. "Grandma likes everything neat!"

Tutter was working hard. He wanted everything to look perfect when his grandma arrived.

In a little while, the otters and Ojo were back. "We got all the weeds!" they shouted.

"And I got a tulip!" added Pop.

Tutter gulped. "You're all muddy!" he said. "And I'm all dirty! And—" *Dingdong!*

Did you hear that?
That was the doorbell!

"Oh, no!" cried Tutter. "It's Grandma Flutter! She's here! What'll we do?"

"I think we'd better answer the door," said Bear.

"Not yet, Bear, I'm not ready yet!" said Tutter.

"Don't worry, Tutter," said Bear. "Everything will be fine."

"Welcome to the Big Blue House, Grandma Flutter," said Bear.

Grandma Flutter looked up—way, way up. "You must be Bear," she said. "I've heard so much about you! And where is that wonderful grandson of mine?"

"He-he-here I am, Grandma," Tutter said. "Uh, if I could just explain. See, we cleaned and cleaned. But the flowers, and the dirt, and . . . oh, hickory dickory!"

"Hush now, Tutter," said Grandma Flutter. "I'm just happy to see you and meet your friends! That's what really matters to me."

"That's right," Bear agreed. "If there's one thing that's true about families, it's that they love each other no matter what."

"No matter what!" said Grandma Flutter. She held her tiny arms
out very wide. "And now, Tutter," she said.

"Yes, Grandma Flutter?" said Tutter.

"Come over here and give your grandma a great big hug."

And he did.